D0422725

Case of the Uncrackable Code

By Kyla Steinkraus

Illustrated by David Ouro

Rourke
Educational Media
rourkeeducationalmedia.com

www.rourkeeducationalmedia.com

Edited by: Keli Sipperley
Cover and interior layout by: Jen Thomas
Cover and Interior Illustrations by: David Ouro

Library of Congress PCN Data

Case of the Uncrackable Code / Kyla Steinkraus
(Rourke's Mystery Chapter Books)
ISBN (hard cover)(alk. paper) 978-1-63430-388-0
ISBN (soft cover) 978-1-63430-488-7
ISBN (e-Book) 978-1-63430-583-9
Library of Congress Control Number: 2015933744

Printed in the United States of America, North Mankato, Minnesota

Dear Parents and Teachers:

With twists and turns and red herrings, readers will enjoy the challenge of Rourke's Mystery Chapter Books. This series set at Watson Elementary School builds a cast of characters that readers quickly feel connected to. Embedded in each mystery are experiences that readers encounter at home or school. Topics of friendship, family, and growing up are featured within each book.

Mysteries open many doors for young readers and turn them into lifelong readers because they can't wait to find out what happens next. Readers build comprehension strategies by searching out clues through close reading in order to solve the mystery.

This genre spreads across many areas of study including history, science, and math. Exploring these topics through mysteries is a great way to engage readers in another area of interest. Reading mysteries relies on looking for patterns and decoding clues that help in learning math skills.

Whether readers are reading the books independently or you are reading with them, engaging with them after they have read the book is still important. We've included several activities at the end of each book to make this both fun and educational.

Do you think you and your reader have what it takes to be a detective? Can you solve the mystery? Will you accept the challenge?

Rourke Educational Media

Table of Contents

Possible Alien Encounter

"Who knows what is so special about next week?" Miss Flores asked.

I raised my hand. "A mega-asteroid is going to hit the moon and school will be canceled for the rest of our lives?"

"Good try, but that's not quite the answer I was looking for, Rocket."

My name is actually Ronald Carson Gonzaga, but everyone calls me Rocket on account of me being the speediest kid around.

My friend Tully raised her hand. "Next week we have both the 100th day of school and Valentine's Day."

Miss Flores smiled. "Right! The 100th day of school is Wednesday, and Valentine's Day is Thursday. For the 100th day of school, I'd like you to put 100 items on an article of clothing to wear to class."

I exchanged grins with Caleb, Lyra, Tully, and Alex, my four best friends and the best detectives at Watson Elementary. We are so good at solving cases we even have a name: the Gumshoe Gang. We do not actually have gum on our shoes. A gumshoe is a detective who solves cases. The school secretary Mr. Sleuth gave us that name way back when we were in second grade.

"Can I glue 100 Hot Wheels cars to my shirt?" Caleb asked. He loves cars and math. He is also really messy.

"What about glass beakers?" asked Alex, pushing his glasses up his nose. Alex was really smart, and he loved science.

Miss Flores frowned. "Unfortunately, I think that would be a safety hazard."

"I'm going to do candy," Aidan said.

"I want to use safety pins!" Maya said.

"I call diamonds!" Tully said. She was very smart and organized, and her favorite thing was to wear lots of weird sparkly outfits.

Lyra raised her hand. "I want to use candy hearts. Can I eat them off my shirt?" Lyra was a great singer, but she had trouble with being too loud sometimes. I did too.

"I'm not sure the glue would taste very good," Miss Flores said. She was the teacher for Room 113, and my favorite teacher ever. "Great ideas, class. Let's break for silent reading. Find your favorite spot."

Most of the class raced for the reading loft. I almost always got there first. Mostly I loved being in third grade, but sometimes it wasn't so much fun because Miss Flores made us read so much. As in, every single day. I am not even joking.

Reading is tough because I have dyslexia, which means I read words backward and mix up letters. Sometimes my eyes get so tired I have to prop them open with toothpicks. Well, not really, but you get the picture.

Because reading is so hard, I couldn't concentrate very well. I opened my book, but the words were fuzzy on the page. So instead I started thinking about the problem of our new computer lab teacher, Mr. Benton. He was what the school principal, Mrs. Holmes, called a long-term sub for Mrs. Joseph. Last week, Mrs. Joseph left to be on something called maternity, on account of having two babies at the same time.

Mr. Benton had a big hairy beard on his face and eyebrows so thick they looked like one long fuzzy caterpillar. He never smiled. He called the cafeteria the "chow hall" and he yelled "Drop and give me 20!" every time he caught someone doing note passing.

He always forgot everybody's name, too. Instead he called us Roger this and Roger that, and the funny thing was we didn't even have a Roger in the whole school! Who knew where he got these things?

I was pretty sure Mr. Benton was an undercover space alien sent to Earth to experiment on the brains of students. Or maybe back on his space ship, he had a hungry alien pet named Froodle who only snacked on third graders. Froodle had twelve spider legs, a body like a fat slimy frog, and a purple poodle head. Don't ask me how I knew this.

The rest of the Gumshoe Gang didn't share my suspicions. In fact, Lyra laughed at me so hard, milk shot out of her nose. And not in the I-can't-believe-how-funny-you-are kind of way. They didn't believe me that totally weird equals possible alien invader.

But I knew better.

A Spy at School

The real trouble started that afternoon. Outside it was cloudy and snowing. We had just finished lunch in the cafeteria. For me, it was the usual rice with some ulam—last night's fish stew.

On Tuesdays and Thursdays, we have computer lab upstairs. All the kids were piling into the classroom. I made sure to get in first so I could shoot my friends with mega-asteroids while shouting "Your planet is doomed!" One of my crumpled wads of paper bounced right off of Carys Johnson's head and rolled under the long row of computer tables.

"Ronald, you stop that right now!" Carys was the only person who called me Ronald. Even Mrs. Holmes agreed Rocket was a better name. It was so annoying I decided to do a double strike on her.

On account of being fresh out of mega-asteroids,

I stooped down to look for the one under the table. Then I crawled under the computer table, wiggling around between all the cords and other kids' legs.

I found it, plus several paper clips, a hard stick of gum, a crumbly pile of stale potato chips, and – Eureka! – a green, chewed-on bouncy ball. Yes, human chewing. I grabbed the bouncy ball and popped a potato chip in my mouth. Still delicious.

"Atten-SHUN!" Mr. Benton bellowed.

I jumped to my feet. Thud! Oops. I was still under the table.

I rubbed my throbbing skull. It felt like getting smacked over the head with a baseball bat. That has actually happened to me. Just ask my big sister Cadence.

Mr. Benton started roll call. He called us by our last names, and he always started with Z, so I still had time.

"Pssst," my friend Braylen hissed, "get in your seat, quick!"

"I'm trying," I whispered back, still holding the side of my head. I yanked aside the computer cords hanging above me like snakes in a jungle. Then I saw it. A folded square of paper was taped

to the underside of the table, right where Maya Heart was sitting. Maya's unlaced sneakers were swinging straight at me, so I had to stretch really far to reach it without getting kicked.

" . . . James . . . "

"Aqui!" Caleb said, showing off the Spanish Miss Flores was teaching us.

I grabbed the folded paper, stuffed it in my back pocket, and crawled toward the empty space between the rows of legs.

"Repeat that?" Mr. Benton asked sternly.

"I mean, here, sir. Sorry, sir."

" . . . Gonzaga . . . "

I hurled myself into my chair. The chair rocked backward and almost toppled over. "Here!" I gasped.

Mr. Benton looked up with narrowed eyes. But I was in my seat, smiling sweetly, just like everybody else.

". . . Heart . . . "

"Here!" Maya said.

"That was a close shaving," Caleb whispered.

I touched my face. "I didn't shave anything. I did smack my head, though."

"You find any of my Hot Wheels cars down there?"

"No, but you won't believe what I did find." I reached for the folded note. I couldn't wait to have somebody read it for me.

Just then Mr. Benton stomped over. He glared at us, his single eyebrow going up and down. "This is a no talking zone, boys. Drop and give me 20!"

Mr. Benton always gave us the choice: we could write 20 sentences, or we could drop right there on the floor and do 20 pushups. It was an easy choice for me. I was quickly becoming the kid with the biggest biceps in the whole third grade.

Secret Messages

After computer lab, we had second recess. We huddled in a circle underneath the slide. The sun was shining. Brown grass peeked through the snow.

I unfolded the note I'd found and set it in the middle of the group. I didn't bother reading it. I was always last to figure the words out anyway. I tossed my new green ball in the air and caught it.

"Why are the letters all jumbled up?" Tully asked.

"It's just nonsense," Caleb said.

"Is this written in another language?" asked Lyra in a confused voice.

I looked to see what all the fuss was about. On the unfolded paper was a message written in blue ink:

– Der Skcos – Eht Stneidergni Era Desahcrup.

Gnixim Hguod Ni Ssergorp. Rewolf Deriuqca.
Elbanu Ot Etacol Etalocohc Spihc. Esaelp Esivda.
– Eulb Skcos –

That's the message my friends saw. I saw something totally different. Instead of having to hunt through every letter to figure out each word, the letters and words clicked together like a puzzle. It was magic. "It's not nonsense!" I said.

"What do you mean?" Lyra asked.

"It's a code."

"Like a secret message!" Alex said excitedly.

"Yes!" I pointed at the letters. "The letters are scrambled backward in each word so it's hard to understand for anyone who doesn't know the code."

"Well, that's great. But how are we going to figure it out?" Tully asked.

I couldn't have kept the huge grin off my face if I'd tried. "I already did."

"What?!" everybody said at the same time.

"Jinx!" I yelled. Then I had to say each person's name a bunch of times so they could tell me how amazed they were at my code-cracking skills.

Lyra clapped her hands. "Tell us what it says!"

I ran my finger beneath each word as I read: "Red Socks. The ingredients are purchased. Mixing dough in progress. Flower acquired. Unable to locate chocolate chips. Please advise. Blue Socks."

"A secret message about cooking?" Caleb smacked his own head. "Ugh!"

"Spies say things like flour, dough, and chocolate chips, but they mean something else," I explained. "They use special code words, so they can talk about spying and everybody thinks they're talking about baking."

"But how are we going to figure it out?" Caleb asked.

Tully pulled her notebook out of her purple

fur coat. It was a yellow polka-dotted notebook with REAL DETECTIVE CLUES: PRIVATE NO PEEKING scrawled in purple marker, with THAT MEANS YOU! written at the bottom. "We'll analyze it for clues, just like our other cases."

Miss Flores blew her whistle. "Recess is over!"

Tully tucked the note in her pocket as we crawled out from under the slide.

"You peed your pants!" Caleb yelled and pointed at Lyra. Lyra, Alex, and Tully all had wet circles on their pants.

"Tully needs a diaper!" I said, giggling.

Tully and Lyra crossed their arms and stared at us in disgust. "Seriously?" Tully said in a snippy voice. "You clowns know that you were doing the exact same thing as us, right? Our pants are wet from the snow."

I patted my own bottom. Oops. "Ha ha. Good joke, right?"

The girls rolled their eyes at me. They always forgot I had built-up immunity from all head shaking/eye rolling/ silent treatments on account of having an older sister.

We trudged toward the school. The girls walked

behind us acting like they were mad. "You know what this means," I said extra loud. "I found the secret message in Mr. Benton's computer lab. Mr. Benton is either a spy, or an alien, or my favorite: a super top-secret alien spy."

We had to wait until the next day at lunch to discuss the meaning of the secret message. Lyra thought the ingredients were for cookies. Caleb was sure it was for muffins. Alex believed the ingredients were for something called scones.

"What are scones," I asked. "Skittles in a cone?"

"No, it's something British," Alex said, which was not helpful at all.

Then we decided it was better to focus on the code names: Red Socks and Blue Socks. We studied everybody's feet all day, only we started running into walls and doors because we couldn't watch where we were going. And it ended up not being helpful at all, on account of the weather still being so cold. All the kids including us were covered up in boots and long pants. I didn't even know what color my own socks were.

"How can you not know that? Don't you dress yourself in the morning?" Tully said with more eye rolling and sighs.

We were all frustrated. What if we couldn't figure it out?

Invisible Spies

Another long day passed before we had computer lab again. When lunch period was almost over, I threw away my trash and asked for a hall pass. As soon as I was out of sight, I zoomed up two flights of stairs to the second floor.

I was hoping the lab was empty, but Mr. Benton looked up from his desk when I rushed in. He had a book in his hand and a plate covered in crumbs on his desk. He looked at me for a second like he was going to say something, then he just went back to his book. I could hardly see through his bristly beard to tell whether he was happy or annoyed. The eyebrow voted for annoyed.

But he didn't stop me, so I ducked under the tables and crawled around. My arm got snagged in one of the cords for a few seconds, but I managed to escape and made my way to Maya's seat. A square of paper was taped to the underside of the table! My heart did a little dance inside my chest. I grabbed the paper, crawled out, and raced back down the two flights of stairs to the cafeteria.

"Aha!" I said, dropping it on our table.

"Shhh!" Lyra said, which was a big surprise coming from her. "What if the real spy is watching?"

Good point. We crowded in tight, so no one else could see. Tully used her fingertips and carefully unfolded the paper. "Is this a joke?"

The paper was blank. As in, there was nothing on it. No writing or typing or drawings or anything. I felt sick, like I'd just swallowed a smelly sneaker.

"This isn't funny, Rocket," Alex said.

I lifted my shoulders and held out my hands, trying to show them I was as shocked as they were. "I didn't do anything, I promise."

The bell rang. Caleb pushed out his chair. "Nice try, Rocket. You can't pull the sheep over our eyes!"

"I'm not making this up!"

Tully narrowed her eyes. "Doesn't it seem a little strange that you found both notes, AND you deciphered the code before any of us?"

A wave of kids rushed past us toward the stairs. I couldn't move. "You think I'm lying?"

"You want us to think Mr. Benton is an alien, or a spy, or whatever," Lyra said, crossing her arms over her chest.

I didn't even correct her that he was probably both. The sick feeling inside me got worse. My friends thought I was making it up. "Fine, then!"

"You've buttered your bread, now lie in it," Caleb said.

"That doesn't even mean anything!" I yelled after him, but Caleb, Lyra, and Tully were already walking away.

My eyes started to get wet and I had to blink a bunch of times. I grabbed the blank paper and stuffed it in my pocket. I wasn't ready to give up hope just yet.

In the computer lab, Mr. Benton had us open the writing program called Word on our computers. He taught us how to compose a formal letter. We were supposed to type things like "to whom it may concern," "thank you for your consideration," and "sincerely," and include dates and addresses and stuff. I wanted to type, "Dear Sirs and Madams of the Gumshoe Gang, you are all terrible friends. Thank you for your consideration. Sincerely, Rocket. P.S. I am the best detective."

But it would take me longer than the whole class period to type all those words in the right order. I had another idea instead. I clicked on Google. I glanced over the top of my computer. Mr. Benton was still pacing back and forth at the front of the classroom.

I typed in blank paper and spy message, but I messed up a bunch of times before I got it right. My insides felt all jumpy, like I had frogs hopping around in my stomach.

The very first result to pop up looked like it spelled inbivisle nik, but then my brain unscrambled itself. I'd just solved the mystery of the blank message! It was written in invisible ink. One spy wrote a message in lemon juice, which disappeared on the paper, until the second spy held it up to something really hot. Eureka!

Next to me, I heard Caleb gasp. At first I thought he'd seen what was on my computer screen. Then I realized no one was talking. Every kid in the room was looking straight at me.

Suddenly Mr. Benton loomed above me. "What exactly are you doing, Mr. Gonzaga?"

I stared at my shaking hands. I couldn't look up. What if all of a sudden everybody realized the reason Mr. Benton never smiled was because he had huge slobbering fangs? And what if right that second he was preparing to inhale me for lunch, or crack open my head and inspect my brains, or—

"We need to have a conversation, sir," Mr. Benton growled. "I am writing you a detention slip. However, I have a meeting today, so I will see you tomorrow at 1500 hours."

I wanted to yell, "But I don't even know what time that is!" But Mr. Benton had already moved back to the front of the room.

Secret Agent Guy

I slumped in my seat and tried to keep the tears from coming out for the second time in less than an hour. Getting embarrassed in front of everybody was bad. Getting caught breaking the rules was bad. Almost getting eaten by my teacher was pretty awful too. On top of that: detention. But none of that was the worst thing. The worst thing was what would happen when my mother found out.

Mom would do what she did every other time I got detention: sit in Mr. Sleuth's office and huff and mutter things to herself in Filipino, phrases which probably meant "My son is so disappointing" and "Why can't he be more like his sister, who is perfect in every way?" I pretended she meant "My son is the brightest star among all of his 17 cousins. He is most likely destined to be knighted by the Queen of England!"

Anyway, I didn't want to think about all that. I had plenty of troubles piled high on my plate already. This day was all wrong. Everything was so upside down it was making me feel sick to my stomach. I raised my hand for a hall pass. Mr. Benton lifted his bushy eyebrow, but he let me go.

On the way to the bathroom, I passed a fifth grader named Travis. Lyra called him Travis the Terrible, on account of him being really mean sometimes. "Hey Shorty, what's up?"

"My name is Rocket," I said.

He just laughed and ruffled my hair, which I hated. I pushed his hand away.

"Hey! What's your problem, squirt?"

I kept walking. I couldn't handle any other bad things today. If Caleb was here, he would say something funny to get Travis to stomp off in a huff. But Caleb wasn't talking to me right now.

That's when I ran into Mr. Sleuth. I mean, my eyes were stinging and watery, and I actually ran into him. My head smacked into his elbow. I bounced backward and fell flat on my butt. "Ouch!"

"Fiddlesticks!" Mr. Sleuth cried. He was so tall he had to stoop almost sideways to help me up. "My apologies, my boy. I didn't even see you down there. Hey now, what's the matter?"

"Allergies," I sniffed, but we both knew that wasn't true. And then somehow I was telling Mr. Sleuth everything that was going wrong, including scary Mr. Benton, detention, my mean friends, and the secret messages.

"Hmmm," Mr. Sleuth said after a long moment. He stroked his chin. "I can't help solve all of your problems, but I might be able to help you with a few. If we hurry, we can get you back to class in a jiffy."

I had no idea what a jiffy was, but I followed Mr. Sleuth downstairs to his office. He turned on the lamp sitting on his desk and took off the lampshade. "Hold your blank paper up to the light bulb for a minute."

I did. Slowly letters appeared on the paper, sort of a stained brown color, but it was definitely a message. Eureka! I had the next clue in the case! But even better, the Gumshoe Gang had to believe me now! I would get my friends back. Suddenly my upside-down day was turning right side up. Or

at least sideways. I hugged Mr. Sleuth and raced back to the computer lab.

The only problem was, I didn't get a chance to talk to my friends for the rest of the day. And as soon as I got home, I was grounded. No TV or iPad or playing with Legos. I had to pick up all my toys that had somehow gotten all over the house, plus sweep the whole floor. Cadence stuck her tongue out at me, smirking every chance she got. For being a fifth grader, she was not as mature as everybody thought she was.

Because of all that cleaning, I almost didn't have time to finish making my 100th Day shirt. I found a black Sharpie marker and a white shirt. I drew a fat alien face with a toothy grimace down at the bottom. On the rest of the face, I glued 100 differently sized googly eyes. Above all the eyes, I put one long bushy eyebrow. It looked pretty fantastic.

On Wednesday morning, I got to Room 113 late because Cadence had to change her hairdo 12 times. Ugh. Sisters.

It was first recess before I got a chance to talk to my friends. Alex, Tully, and Lyra were tugging on their coats while Caleb tried to shove his locker shut. Stuff kept spilling out: a lunch box, books, a ruler, crumpled homework, and the petri dish we used for a mold experiment way back in October.

Lyra squealed and jumped back. "That's so disgusting!"

"Guys. We need to talk," I said. I decided to have grace under pressure. "Also, I forgive you." They stared at me until I very secretively showed them the blank message that wasn't blank anymore.

Tully gasped.

Caleb grinned at me like we were best friends again, which we were. It couldn't have gone better if I'd planned it, which I sort of spent all last night doing. "Your alien shirt is totally awesome."

"So are your cars," I said. He'd plastered 100 race car stickers all over his shirt.

Lyra wrapped her arms around me. "I'm so sorry, Rocket! You were right!"

Alex cleared his throat. "You were right about some things. Mr. Benton is still not an alien."

"That has not been proven, yet," I said, and pointed at my shirt.

Caleb burst out laughing. And all was right with the world again.

The Dead Drop

By the time we were all friends again, most of the other kids were already on the playground. "Hurry up, please!" Miss Flores called to us from the front door.

"Let's read the message," Tully said as we walked. I handed it to her. She read aloud: "Red Socks. Did not receive last transmission. Possible burnt toast. Repeat: Cookies ready for oven. Flower acquired and access confirmed. Must meet to relocate dead drop: observation point at the North Pole. Wednesday. 200. Blue Socks."

"Toast?" Caleb cried, throwing up his hands. "What does toast have to do with cookies?"

"Or flowers," Alex said.

Tully opened the front door. A blast of cold air hit us as we hurried outside. The sun was shining, and the snow sparkled so bright it hurt my eyes.

We crowded in close to each other.

"What does 'dead drop' mean?" Lyra asked. "That sounds bad."

"I agree," Alex said grimly.

"What if toast means something bad too?" Caleb asked. "Like 'you're toast!' means somebody's out to get you?"

I started getting nervous. "What if the clues are all about food because the spies are really undercover aliens who want to chomp us up like we're giant gooey cookies?"

Tully pulled her notebook and a pencil out of her back pocket. "Okay, everybody calm down. In the last clue, the spy also spelled flour 'flower' like the plant, not 'flour' like the baking ingredient."

Caleb and I looked at her. "Huh?"

"What if flower is a code name, like we know Blue Socks and Red Socks are code names?"

We all thought quietly for a minute, listening to the laughter and shouting on the playground. "What if flower is a code name for Miss Flores?" Lyra said.

All of our eyes lit up at that big Aha! moment. Miss Flores' name means flower in Spanish! Caleb said what all of us were thinking: "Does that mean Miss Flores is in danger?"

No one wanted to answer that question. Tully tapped the secret message with her pen. "If so, it's even more important we figure this out. First, we need to focus on the meeting. It says Wednesday, which is today. 1400 hours means two o'clock."

How come everybody knows this weird hundreds of hours stuff except for me? I thought to myself.

"The clue says 'observation point at the North Pole'." Alex frowned. "The North Pole is way up north. It has a pole in its name. Santa's shop is at the North Pole."

"The North Pole is super cold." I rubbed my mittens together. "And so am I."

"Great idea, Rocket. Maybe the North Pole is outside." Alex turned and looked at the playground. "And the observation point could be a . . . a bench, like that one right there?"

"Yes!" I hollered. Because sitting at the very bench that Alex was pointing at was someone I knew all too well. Maya Heart, the girl who sat right at the spot where I'd found the last two secret messages. "She must be one of the spies!"

I was so excited I thought I might burst right out of my skin, just like an alien. A real live spy at school!

"We need to trick her," Tully said. "One of us pretends to be the other spy. Use the code words from the messages to get the spy to reveal something important."

"I'll do it!" Caleb volunteered. We made our plan. Caleb would sit next to Maya and act like a spy. Tully and I would pretend to build a snowman a little ways from the bench. Only we'd be doing double duty and listening in on the talk. Alex and Lyra would walk around the playground, searching for the second spy. It was a perfect spy plan.

Caleb sat next to Maya. He sighed and stretched his legs. "It's a great day to bake some cookies, don't you think?"

"Oh sure," Maya said. "Cookies sound yummy. What kind?"

"Chocolate chip."

"Oh, that's my favorite."

"Does the cookie need to go to the doctor?"

Caleb asked in a low, serious voice.

"Um, what?"

"Maybe he is feeling crummy."

"Oh. Ha ha."

"Who else is feeling crummy?"

"What do you mean?"

"Are the cookies burnt? Did you burn them?"

"Wait—what are we talking about?"

"You're a smart cookie. You figure it out."

"What?" Maya stood up with her hands on her hips.

"It's all or muffin, Maya."

"I didn't burn any cookies or muffins! Or toast! I don't know what you're thinking, but you're baking up the wrong tree!" With that, she stomped off toward the playground.

"Donut underestimate me!" Caleb called after her, giggling at his own joke. He looked back at us and shrugged. "She's one tough cookie to crack."

Tully elbowed me. "The cookie is baked! The cookie is baked!"

"Huh?"

"Over there," she hissed, gesturing with her head but keeping her eyes on the snowman.

Someone in a long dark coat was hurrying back toward the school. I could see from the tracks in the snow that the suspect had been walking right toward the bench. The other spy!

"I'll get him!" I leapt to my feet and sprinted after the suspect. I was gaining on him, but he was already almost to the front door. He must have known I was right behind him because he didn't look back even one time.

"Rocket! Come back please!" Miss Flores called from the playground. I stopped in my tracks. The suspect dashed into the school and disappeared. I groaned, but I obeyed. I already had one detention today.

When I got back to my friends, Caleb had a folded up piece of yellow paper in his hand. Another secret message! "I thought I'd check underneath the bench, just in case!" he said proudly.

He opened the message. It said:

YOFV HLXPH, NVVG NVZG NIH S LUURXV. YIRMT GSV XLLPRVH. -IEW HLXPH.

We all stared at it in dismay.

"We're never going to figure it out!" Lyra moaned.

"But at least we know Maya is the spy, right?" I asked.

Alex shook his head. "She didn't act like she knew what you were talking about."

"The message could have been planted earlier, before she sat down," Tully said.

Alex nodded. "She's a red herring."

"Maya's a bird?" I wrinkled up my nose.

"A red herring is a fish," Alex said.

"Maya's a fish?"

"No! It's a metaphor. A red herring is a misleading clue. Maya sat where the notes were taped under the table and she was sitting on the bench where the spies were supposed to meet. Those were clues, but they could be pointing us in the wrong direction."

"Hmmph," Caleb grunted. He didn't sound too sure.

"Mr. Benton may be a red herring, too," Tully said. "The spy messages were in his classroom. That clue might make us think he's one of the spies."

"How do you know he's not?" I muttered.

"The spies probably chose Mr. Benton's room

because he teaches all the students," Alex said. "Everyone uses the lab, so the spies could be in different grades and still send messages to each other."

"Oh. Good point."

"Guys," Tully said. "We should copy this message on another piece of paper and put it back. Then the spies won't know we've found it."

"Great idea," I said.

She copied the jumbled up letters into her notebook. We spread out in front of the bench, blocking the view of any possible spies while Tully put the message back.

Caleb pushed his bangs out of his eyes. "This case is snowballing into a big can of worms!"

"I know." Lyra sat down in the snow and put her head in her hands. "What if this code is uncrackable? What if Miss Flores is really in trouble?" No one wanted to think about that.

The Cookie is Baked

At lunch time, we found our seats in the cafeteria. I traded one of my egg rolls for Alex's peanut butter crackers. Lyra kept pulling the candy hearts off her sleeves and eating them. We were quiet. We had no idea how to crack the uncrackable code.

Caleb tugged little strings off of his string cheese and laid them out on his napkin. It wasn't normal for him not to gulp it up in two bites. "What's up?" I asked him.

He made a face. "I keep thinking about what Maya said. It's bugging me like a fly in my soup."

I pushed away my plate. "Let's talk it through again."

"I asked her about baking cookies, then if the cookie needed to go the doctor. Then I asked if she burned the cookies. She was all confused and upset. I said something about a muffin. She said she didn't burn any cookies, muffins, or toast. Then she said I was 'baking' up the wrong tree. That was pretty funny."

I thought hard about what Maya had said. I imagined a cookie all burnt up and a squishy blueberry muffin with a blackened top. I imagined a slimy green alien stomping them to pieces while he gobbled up a slice of bread. You're toast! Was Maya really innocent? Or had she somehow given herself away? Had she—"Wait! I got it!"

"What?"

I was so excited I could barely keep myself from jumping on top of the table and dancing. "Maya said cookies, muffins and toast! Burnt toast is in the secret message, but Caleb never said anything about toast, only cookies."

"We just caught a real, live spy!" Lyra said.

Only it didn't really work out that way. We found Maya dumping the rest of her lunch into the trash can by the cafeteria doors. "We know it's you!" I said. "Turn yourself in!"

A flutter of panic crossed Maya's face but then she scowled. "You can't prove anything."

"We have two of your secret messages!"

"So?"

"Are you planning on doing something to Miss Flores?" Tully asked.

"Ugh. You guys don't know anything." She turned to walk away.

"We're going to tell Mrs. Holmes!" Lyra said.

"Go right ahead," Maya called over her shoulder.

We just looked at each other. "She's right," Alex said finally. "We don't have enough evidence. Whatever she's doing, we need to catch her in the act. We need to crack that code."

"Yes!" Caleb said. "We must crumble that cookie!"

After school, I had detention. I slumped in my seat, feeling about as crummy as those imaginary burnt up cookies. But then Mr. Benton did a surprising thing. Instead of sitting at his desk and reading, he put his book on the table and sat in the chair next to me. "I think we need to have a chat, Mr. Gonzaga."

I stared at the keyboard. "My name is Rocket."

"I see . . . Rocket. It seems this class has been

difficult for you. Can you tell me why?"

My face felt hot. "I don't know."

"I know I'm probably a little different than the other teachers you've had."

"A little, sir?"

Mr. Benton raised his bristly eyebrow. "Why don't you tell me about it?"

I touched one of the googly eyes on my alien T-shirt. I was tired of dreading computer lab. Plus, my sore arms were even more tired of all those pushups. So I told him how hard the class was for me. "Plus, I think I'm flunking because I had to do like 500 pushups, I don't know what 'latrine' and 'lollygagging' means, and on top of that, I have no idea who Roger is!"

Then Mr. Benton did an even more shocking thing. He burst out laughing. And you know what? He had shiny metal stuff all over his teeth. I am not even joking about that. Mr. Benton had braces!

My mouth dropped wide open. I stared at him.

"I know I'm a little old for it," Mr. Benton said. "But after I was discharged from the Army, I decided it was time to fix my teeth. But now

they're really sore."

"That's why you never smile?"

Mr. Benton shook his head. "I'm not smiling? That's not a good thing, is it? I think the pain in my teeth has made me grumpy. That's my fault, and things are going to change as of right now. What's more, I think we can work together to create some assignments for you that are still challenging but will allow you to finish in class."

Up close, I could see that Mr. Benton really had two eyebrows, not one. All of a sudden he didn't look as scary anymore. "Okay!"

Mr. Benton smiled. Or, at least I think it was a smile. It was still hard to tell through his shaggy beard. "'Roger that' is a military term that means you understand the instructions. So instead of 'okay,' you could say 'Roger that!'"

Oh! Now things were making sense. "Roger that?"

"Exactly."

That's when I saw the cover of Mr. Benton's book. I sounded it out carefully. "Cryptography? Is that another Army thing?"

Mr. Benton picked up the book. "It is, especially during wartime. It's also a hobby of mine. Cryptography is the study of secret codes and how to break them."

Eureka! I almost shot right out of my chair. "Mr. Benton, could you help us crack the uncrackable code?"

"Roger that. I've got your six."

Ugh. Just when I thought I was figuring this guy out.

Cracking the Code

The next day was Valentine's Day. I brought a shoebox of Valentine cards with a picture of a green alien hugging a heart with "You're out of this world!" written on it. They were awesome. It was also awesome that Mr. Benton was a teacher at our school. It turns out he wasn't an alien after all. Another totally awesome thing? The unbreakable code was broken! We were going to catch those spies in the act! We weren't quite sure yet what that act was, though.

We did know that the secret message was written in a Reverse Alphabet code. The alphabet was written normally, starting with A, and then directly underneath it you wrote down the alphabet backward, starting with Z. The A represented a Z, the B represented a Y, and so on. To unscramble the message, you matched up the letters from the backward alphabet in the message to the regular alphabet on the top row. So this:

YOFV HLXPH, NVVG NVZG NIH S LUURXV. YIRMT GSV XLLPRVH. -IEW HLXPH.

Became this:

BLUE SOCKS, MEET ME AT TEN AT MRS H OFFICE. BRING THE COOKIES. -RED SOCKS.

And that was why instead of going to recess like regular kids, we begged Miss Flores to send us to the principal's office. And because Miss Flores liked us so much, she did.

The door to Mr. Sleuth's office was open, but he wasn't at his desk. Mrs. Holmes' door was open too. We could hear voices and stuff being moved. We looked at each other silently and nodded. Then we marched right in.

"You're burnt toast!" Caleb shouted.

Maya and her fellow spy nearly jumped out of their skins. They spun around and stood in front of whatever it was they'd been working on. I couldn't believe my eyes. The other spy was Travis the Terrible!

"I thought I smelled something fishy in here," Caleb said, glaring at Maya.

Travis groaned. "What are you guys doing here?"

"We cracked your last message," I said. "Now surrender!"

"What is your evil spy plan?" Caleb demanded. "To steal all the little kids' Valentine's Day cards? To put baby mice in Miss Flores's desk drawers? Or maybe you're about to spray silly string all over Mrs. Holmes's office! What awful thing are the cookies a code for?"

Maya and Travis just stared at us for a long moment. "The cookies," Maya said finally as she stepped aside, "are not a code. We actually made cookies."

On the floor in front of Mrs. Holmes' desk were loads of plates full of chocolate chip cookies. Each plate was covered with red saran wrap and tied with pretty pink and red ribbons.

I tried to think of something terrible someone could do with so many delicious cookies, but I couldn't think of a single thing. My mouth was watering too much.

"They're for the teachers," Travis said.

"It's a surprise," Maya said. "And we don't want

anyone to find out we did it. That's why we were writing secret codes. And also because it's fun."

"Seriously?" Lyra exclaimed.

Travis shrugged. "We were both at the library one day waiting for our parents to pick us up. Mr. Benton showed me his cryptography book, and I was looking for one in the library that I could borrow. Maya and I started talking about spies and secret codes, and then we decided to try our own. But we needed a mission to make it interesting."

Tully made a face. "But what about how you called flour f-l-o-w-e-r in your messages? We thought that was a code for Miss Flores."

"Oops," Maya said, her cheeks red as a Valentine's heart. "That was just a mistake."

I groaned. This whole time we thought Miss Flores was the target, and it was all because of bad spelling. Hmm. Maybe that's why Miss Flores always made us work so hard to spell things correctly.

"But why did you break into Mrs. Holmes's office?" Caleb asked, still suspicious.

"We didn't. Mrs. Holmes wrote us an excuse to get out of classes whenever we need to today.

We have a schedule for all the teachers' recesses and lunch periods, so we can sneak into their classrooms when they're empty."

"Where is Mrs. Holmes anyway?"

Travis sighed and crossed his arms. "She and Mr. Sleuth are decorating the cafeteria with streamers and hearts and stuff. Are you happy now?"

"Well . . . not quite," Lyra said.

Maya stared at us for a minute, chewing her lip like she was deciding something. "Oh all right. Do you want to help?"

"Of course we do!" I said happily.

We held out our hands and Travis gave us each a plate of cookies. "The teacher's name and room number are on the card."

"Okay, guys," Caleb said as we carried the cookies to room 113, "all this talk about cookies is making me hungry. Hungry for a joke, I mean!"

"Tell us," Tully said.

"Two cookies are in an oven. One says 'Boy, it's hot in here.' The other one says, 'Holy moly, a talking cookie!'"

Our laughter echoed all the way down the hallway.

A Peek inside Tully's Notebook:

– Der Skcos – Eht Stneidergni Era Desahcrup.
Gnixim Hguod Ni Ssergorp. Rewolf Deriuqca.
Elbanu Ot Etacol Etalocohc Spihc Esaelp
Esivda. – Eulb Skcos –

Danger? Mission: Save Mrs. Flores!

Suspects List:
1) Mr. Benton
2) Maya
3) Mysterious Spy in the Brown coat (Unknown)

Suspects Found Guilty of Kindness

Q & A with Travis

Rocket: I was shocked when we found you actually doing something nice. I mean, you are Travis the Terrible. Can you explain your motive?

Travis: Hey, I do nice things, squirt. When Maya saw me looking at code books at the library, she really wanted to try one. I thought it was an okay idea for a third grader.

Rocket: Why did you tape the messages underneath the computer lab table?

Travis: Maya sits there during her class, and I sit one seat over during my lab time. It was the perfect way to pass messages.

Rocket: What is up with your code names? We couldn't figure it out.

Travis: That's simple. We just picked our socks colors. I wanted the name Stinky Socks, but Maya said no.

Rocket: That's a great code name.

Travis: Thanks. See you later, short stuff!

Discussion Questions

1. Rocket has dyslexia. How does this make reading harder for him?
2. Why did the Gumshoe Gang think Rocket was making up the secret codes?
3. Why did Mr. Benton seem mean to Rocket when he really wasn't?
4. Why did Maya and Travis use coded messages?
5. How did Rocket figure out that Maya was one of the "spies"?

Writing Prompt

Create two characters who want to keep a secret but need to talk about it with each other. Give them code names, a code to use, and of course, the secret message!

Vocabulary

Here are some important words in the story. Try to write a song using at least five of the vocabulary words.

analyze: to examine something carefully in order to understand it

decipher: to figure out something that is written in code

dyslexia: a person sees letters in the wrong order, making reading difficult

nonsense: talk, writing, or behavior that is silly or annoying

plant: to put something firmly in place

red herring: something that distracts a person from the real issue

sheepish: to look or act embarrassed or ashamed

spy: to watch someone or something secretly to collect information

stomp: to walk heavily or loudly

undercover: to act secretly in a hidden method

Websites to Visit

Practice cracking codes:
https://www.cia.gov/kids-page/games/break-the-code

Write your own secret message in invisible ink:
www.sciencekids.co.nz/experiments/invisibleink.html

Play code-cracking games:
www.nsa.gov/kids/home.shtml

About the Author

Kyla Steinkraus loves mysteries and third graders (she happens to have one at home), so writing books for this series was a perfect fit. She and her two awesome kids love to  snuggle up and read good books together. Kyla also loves playing games, laughing at funny jokes, and eating anything with chocolate in it.

About the Illustrator

I have always loved drawing from a very young age. While I was at school, most of my time was spent drawing comics and copying my favorite characters. With a portfolio under my arm, I started drawing comics  for newspapers and fanzines. After I finished my studies I decided to try to make a living as a freelance illustrator... and here I am!